The Little Reindeer

For my wife, Louise, who told me about the Little Reindeer.

A Red Fox Book

Published by Random House Children's Books
20 Vauxhall Bridge Road, London SW1V 2SA
A division of Random House UK Ltd
London Melbourne Sydney Auckland
Johannesburg and agencies throughout the world

Copyright © Michael Foreman 1996

3 5 7 9 10 8 6 4 2

First published in Great Britain by Andersen Press Ltd 1996

Red Fox edition 1999

Printed in Hong Kong

RANDOM HOUSE UK Limited Reg. No. 954009

ISBN 0 09 940068 5

The Little Reindeer

Michael Foreman

RED FOX

THE little reindeer wondered what all the fuss was about.
He could see lights blazing in the windows of the snow
covered buildings. Shadowy figures rushed in and out of
doorways carrying mysterious bundles.

The little reindeer picked his way through the deep snow towards the biggest building. As he got closer he could hear singing and banging, whirring and rustling.

The little reindeer peeped round the door into the warm, noisy room.

Amazing animals were streaming between rows of singing people. The little reindeer moved further into the room and suddenly found himself being carried along amongst the rest of the animals.

He tried to back away but was pushed forwards by the animals pressing from behind. Suddenly they all disappeared in a blizzard of coloured paper.

He was turned over and over in
swirling colours. Then it went black
and cold and things bumped down
on him until he couldn't move.

He heard jingling bells and
cheering and he felt a great whoosh.

For hours they seemed to stop and start and swoop up and down
until he was tumbling head over hoofs again.

He tried to move his legs, and managed to stand up. Although he was relieved to feel the softness of snow beneath his hoofs, he still couldn't see anything. The little reindeer stood in the darkness, surrounded by strange sounds. Then he heard footsteps crunching towards him.

Suddenly he found himself staring at an astonished face, and then a smile.

"Wow! What a present!" The boy picked him up and danced round and round in the snow.

"But where can I keep you? There are no
pets allowed in the building. I know… You
can stay up here with my pigeons."
    The boy opened the door of a large shed
at one end of the roof. Immediately
the sky filled with birds.

In a corner of the shed
the boy made a straw bed for
the reindeer and fetched milk
and a whole assortment of cereals.
"Tomorrow we can try lots of different
things to eat and see which you like best."
Two by two the pigeons returned to their
perches. They didn't seem to mind the
new visitor.

On Christmas Eve the boy gave the reindeer his favourite dinner and the pigeons sang. They were still singing when he kissed the reindeer goodnight.

From his bed, he thought he heard jingling bells,
but he was probably dreaming by then.

Next morning he rushed up to the
roof but the reindeer had gone. There
were sleigh tracks in the snow. When
he opened the shed and all the pigeons
flew out the boy saw that each had a
red ribbon collar and a little jingle bell.
In the reindeer's bed of straw was a note -
  "Dear Boy,
          Thank you for looking after my
smallest reindeer. See you next year.
     Love,
     Santa Claus."

Through the next spring, summer and autumn the boy heard
the tinkling and jingling of bells each time the pigeons flew.
And on Christmas Eve, when he heard the real jingle bells
coming down from the snowy sky, he was waiting on the
roof with milk and peanut butter sandwiches.